BEST in SHOW

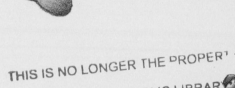

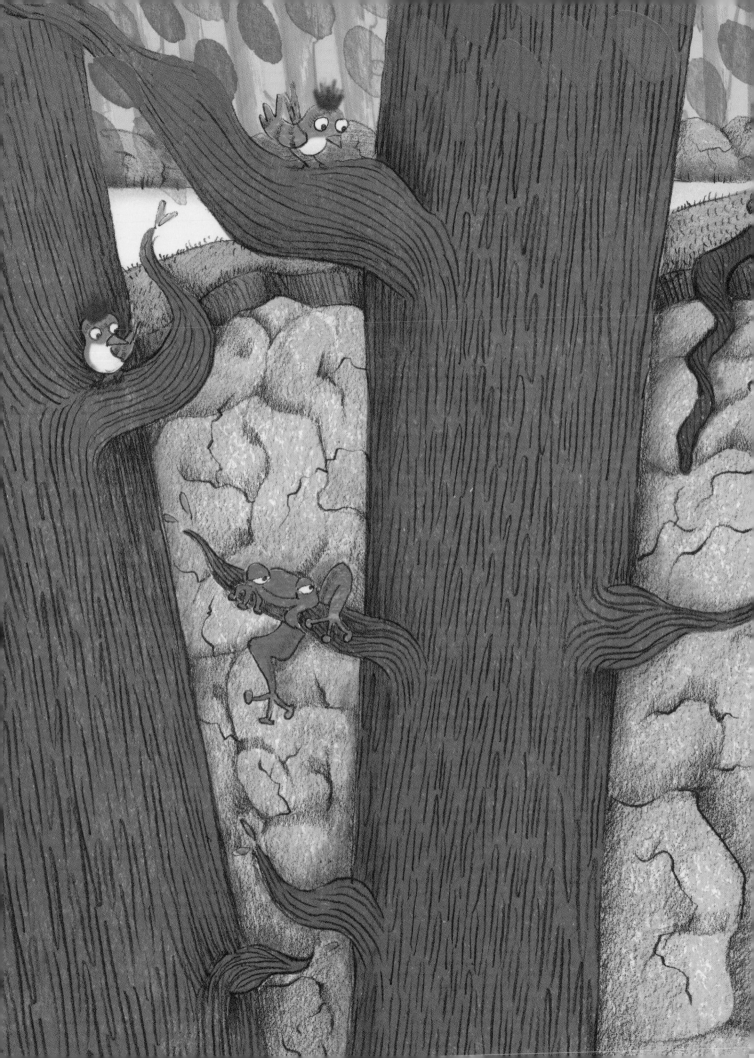

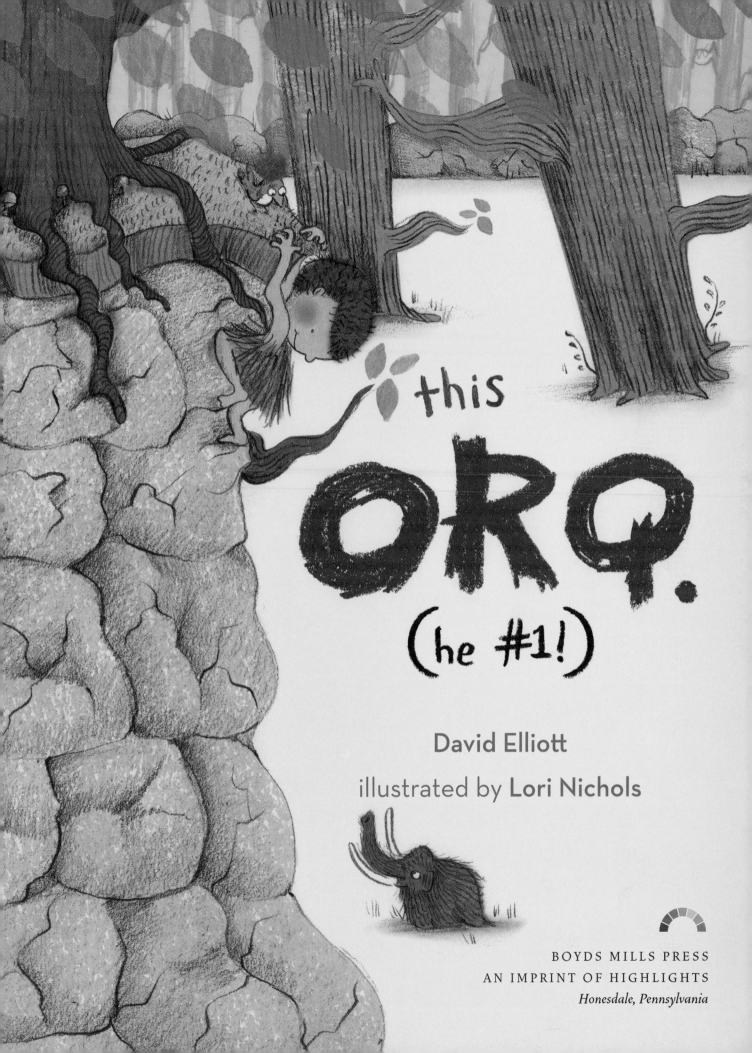

this
ORQ.
(he #1!)

David Elliott

illustrated by Lori Nichols

BOYDS MILLS PRESS
AN IMPRINT OF HIGHLIGHTS
Honesdale, Pennsylvania

For Dan Venecek and Linda Zollo.
They great friends.
—DE

This book for Rachel. She niece.
Fast at track and field. Everybody think so.
—LN

Boyds Mills Press
An Imprint of Highlights
815 Church Street
Honesdale, Pennsylvania 18431

Printed in China
ISBN: 978-1-62979-336-8
Library of Congress Control Number: 2015958464

First edition

Designed by Anahid Hamparian
Production by Sue Cole
The text of this book is set in Neutraface.
The illustrations are done in #4 pencil
on Strathmore drawing paper
and colorized digitally.
10 9 8 7 6 5 4 3 2 1

This Orq.

He cave boy.

Throw far.
Climb high.
Run fast.

This Woma.

He cave boy pet.

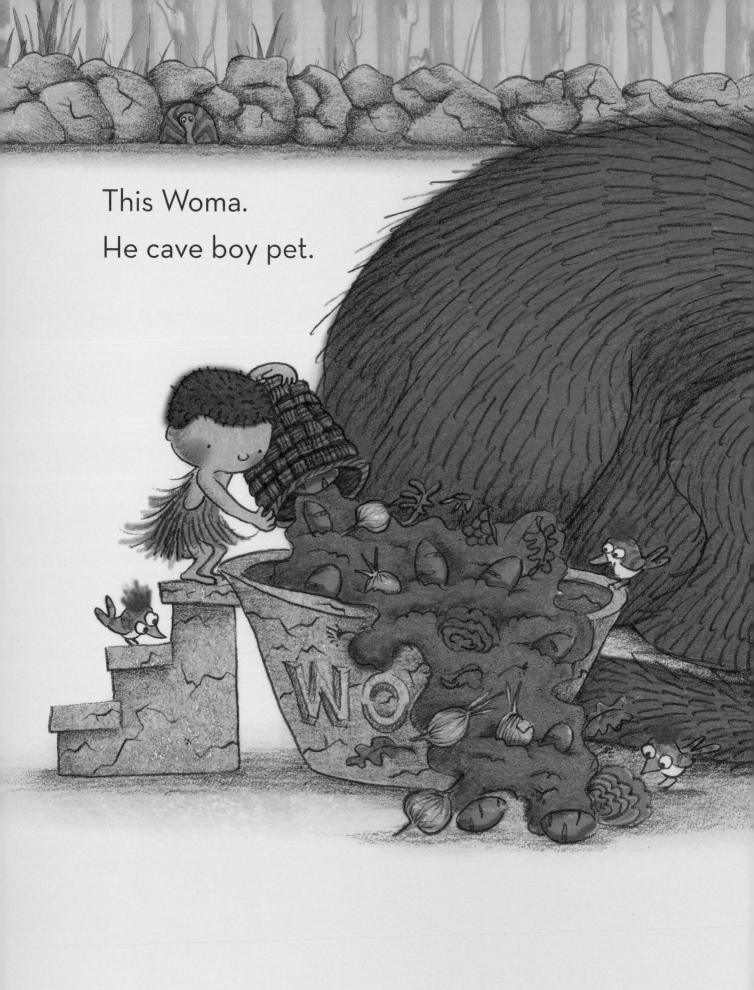

Sleep lots.

Eat tons.

Love plenty.

Orq and Woma #1.
Everybody think so.

Until . . .

. . . Torq and Slomo move into cave next door.

Orq throw.

Torq throw farther!

Orq climb!

Torq climb higher!

Orq run.

Torq . . .

You get picture: Torq #1 now.
Everybody think so.

Especially Torq!

And what so great about Slomo, anyway?

Orq's mother say, "No need to fret, darling. Nobody's best at everything."

Nobody except Torq!
Torq perfect.
Everybody think so.

Especially Torq.

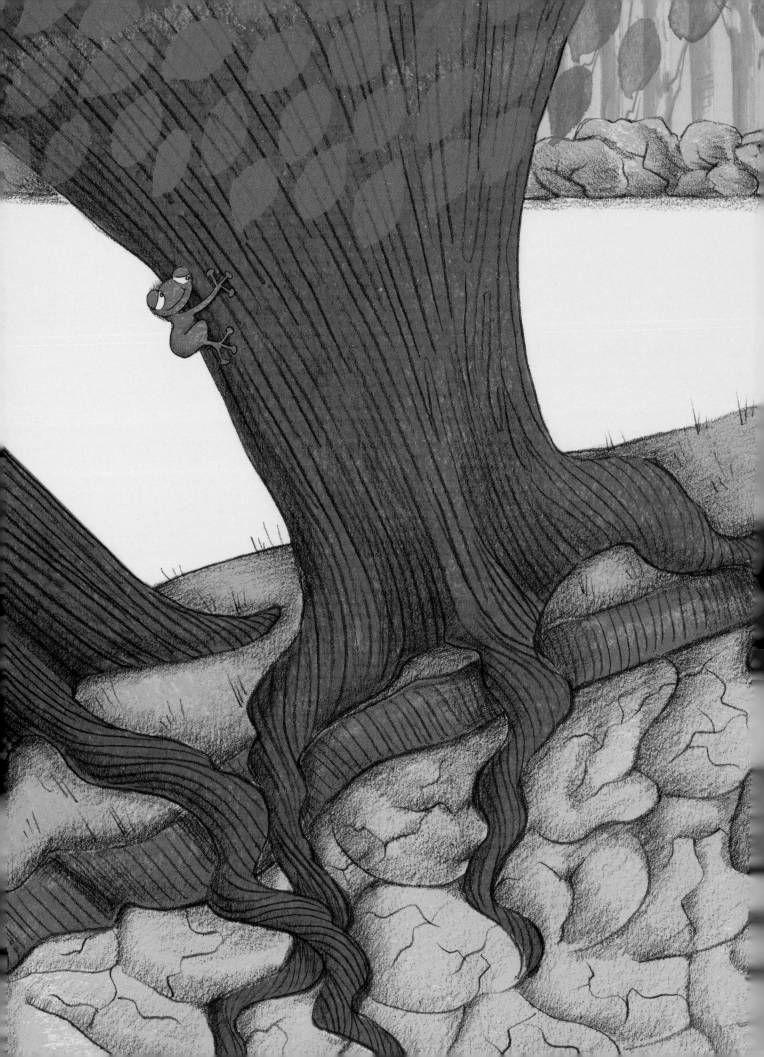

One day, play explorer.

Hike far from cave.

Climb high mountain.

Torq and Slomo at it again.

Oh no!

Ankle swelling.
Night coming.
Orq thinking.

Slomo snoring.

Orq get busy.

Woma help.

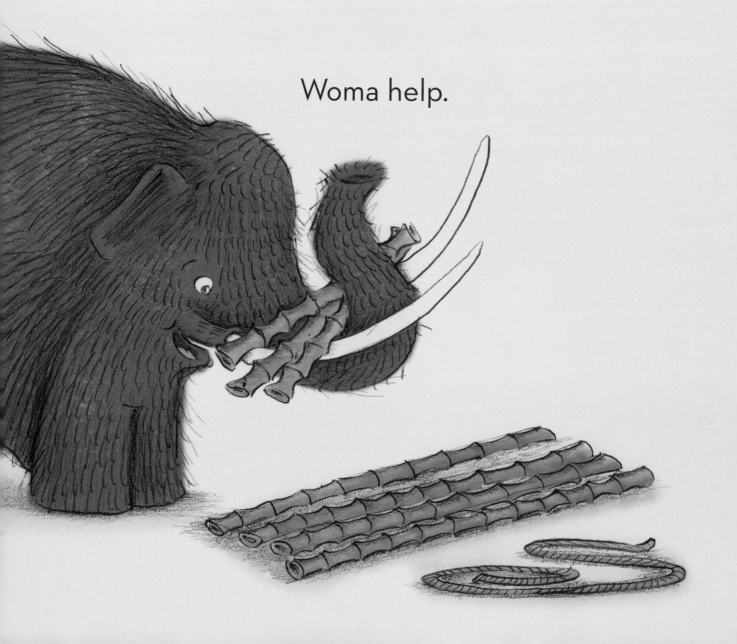

Ta-da!

Orq invent wheel!

Upsee-daisy!

Everybody safe now.

Orq great inventor.

Woma great inventor's helper.

Orq and Woma #1 again.
#1 heroes, that is.

Everybody think so.

Especially Torq.